The Mugged Pug

DARREL & SALLY ODGERS

JACK RUSSELL: Dog Detective

Book #1 DOG DEN MYSTERY

Book #2 THE PHANTOM MUDDER

Book #3 THE MUGGED PUG

Book #4 THE LYING POSTMAN

First American Edition 2007
by Kane/Miller Book Publishers, Inc.
La Jolla, California

First published by Scholastic Press in 2005

Cover photographs by Michael Bagnall
Dog, Sam, courtesy of Glenda Gould
Interior illustrations by Janine Dawson

Kane/Miller Book Publishers, Inc.
P.O. Box 8515
La Jolla, CA 92038
www.kanemiller.com

Library of Congress Control Number: 2006931565
Printed and bound in China
1 2 3 4 5 6 7 8 9 10

ISBN: 978-1-933605-32-6

Dear Readers,

The story you're about to read is about me and my friends, and how we solved The Case of the Mugged Pug. To save time, I'll introduce us all to you now. Of course, if you know us already, you can trot off to the first chapter.

I am Jack Russell, Dog Detective. I live with my landlord, Sarge, in Doggeroo. Sarge detects human-type crimes. I detect the crimes that deal with dogs. I'm a Jack Russell terrier, so I am dogged and intelligent.

Next door to Sarge and me live Auntie Tidge and Foxie. Auntie Tidge is lovely. She has biscuits. Foxie is not lovely. He's a fox terrier (more or less).

He used to be a street dog, and a thief, but he's reformed now. Auntie Tidge has even got rid of his fleas. Foxie sometimes helps me with my cases.

Uptown Lord Setter (Lord Red for short) lives in Uptown House with Caterina Smith. Lord Red means well, but he isn't very bright.

We have other friends and acquaintances in Doggeroo. These include Polly the dachshund, Jill Russell, the Squekes, Fat Molly Cat and Shuffle the pug.

That's all you need to know, so let's get on with the first chapter.

Yours doggedly,

Jack Russell – the detective with a nose for crime.

Terrier-phone

Sarge and I were about to go for our Saturday walk when the **terrier-phone** rang.

"I'd better get that, Jack," said Sarge. "It might be important."

I disagreed. Nothing is more important than Saturday walks, except food.

I **jack-attacked** Sarge's trouser leg to remind him, but Sarge went back into the house.

Since I was hanging on to his trousers by my teeth, I went too.

Sarge picked up the terrier-phone.

I stopped jack-attacking his trousers long enough to find out who was calling.

It was Ranger Jack.

Don't ask me why Doggeroo Dog Control Officer Johnny Wolf calls himself *Ranger Jack*. He just does.

"Straying dogs aren't police business, Ranger Jack," said Sarge to the terrier-phone. "It sounds like Walter Barkly's business to me."

Not police business? Then Sarge and I could go for our walk. I trotted to the door.

"Can't you keep him at the pound until Walter comes back?" asked Sarge. "Oh."

I yapped to remind Sarge that we had important things to do.

"I'll come now," said Sarge.

About time, too!

Sarge unhooked my leash, then he bent and undid my collar. "Sorry, Jack, I need this collar for someone else. You'll have to stay at home."

I didn't believe it. Sarge was giving away my *collar*? How could he?

Jack's Facts

My collar is old and comfortable.
It has my name on it. It smells like me.
My collar is perfect. It is **mine**.
This is a fact.

I jack-attacked Sarge's trouser leg again, but he just shook his head.

"Sorry, Jack," he said.

Sorry? He was taking away my own special collar and he was *sorry*?

After Sarge left, I went to visit Foxie and Auntie Tidge. Auntie Tidge was making **special biscuits**. Foxie was watching, scratching his ribs and drooling.

"How's Jackie-wackie today?" Auntie Tidge is the only person who calls me that.

I whined, to show her how **pawly** I'd been treated. She bent down to pick me up. I gave her a slurp up her cheek that knocked her glasses sideways. She loves it when I do that.

"What are you after, Jack?" snarled Foxie. "This is *my* **terrier-tory**."

I ignored that. Foxie wouldn't even have a terrier-tory if I hadn't arranged for him to live with Auntie Tidge. He wouldn't have a new red collar, either.

"Where's your collar?" asked Foxie, still scratching. "Sarge will be **pawfully** upset if you've lost it."

"He's putting it on someone else," I growled.

"Why?" asked Foxie.

"How should I know?"

Foxie attacked the end of his tail

with his teeth. He hasn't got fleas now, but he has a **terrier-able** time getting rid of the old habit. "Thought you called yourself a detective," said Foxie through a mouthful of imaginary fleas.

I bristled. "I don't *call* myself a detective," I said. "I *am* a detective."

Jack's Glossary

Terrier-phones. *Things that ring.*

Jack-attack. *Growling and biting and worrying at trouser legs. Very loud. Quite harmless.*

Special biscuits. *Auntie Tidge makes these. They don't harm terrier teeth.*

Jack's Glossary

Pawly. *Poorly, badly.*

Terrier-tory. *Territory owned by a terrier.*

Pawfully. *Very.*

Terrier-able. *Same as terrible, but to do with terriers.*

Sarge had taken the car to wherever he had gone. I'm the best tracking Jack in the business, but I knew I wouldn't be **pupular** if I went out without my collar.

<u>*Jack's Facts*</u>

Special dogs need special people.
A special collar says a dog has a special person.
Dogs without special people can end up in the pound.
This is a fact.

"*You* go," I said to Foxie. "You're my second-in-command."

"Go where?" Foxie was still working on that itch.

"Follow Sarge," I said.

Foxie scratched his ear. "Send Red," he said.

I started giving Foxie all the reasons why I couldn't send Red to spy on Sarge. I still hadn't finished when we heard Sarge come back.

I jumped up. By the time Sarge reached the gate, I was lying in my basket with my nose on my paws. I sighed, loudly.

Jack's Facts

When you have been badly treated, you have to show it.
If you don't show the way you feel, no one will be sorry for you.
This is a fact.

"Cheer up, Jack," said Sarge. "I've brought you a visitor." Shuffle the pug followed Sarge. He was wheezing loudly. He was wearing *my* collar. The one I had had for three years. The one with my name on it.

"What are you doing here?" I yapped. "You belong down near the reserve with Walter Barkly."

Shuffle snuffled, then plunked down with his jaw on his paws.

Jack's Facts

Most dogs lie with their noses on their paws.
Pugs have their noses in a different place.
Therefore, pugs lie with their jaws on their paws.
This is a fact.

"Well?" I asked. No Jack wants a pug moving into his terrier-tory without **pawmission**. Especially when the pug is wearing the Jack's collar. I had a bad feeling about this. Shuffle knew he should have asked pawmission to enter my terrier-tory. He hadn't. So something was very wrong.

Shuffle sighed. "I've had a horrible day."

So had I, but at least now I was interviewing a witness. Or a suspect. Or maybe both. I began my **in-terrier-gation**.

"Why are you wearing my collar?"

"Ranger Jack caught me without my collar," snuffled Shuffle. "He took me to the pound. It was horrible, Jack!"

I thought about Shuffle's collar. It is

a new bright blue one, with a silver pug ornament. *I* wouldn't wear it, but Shuffle thinks it's **pawfect.**

"Why didn't Walter Barkly come and get you?" I asked.

"Walter Barkly is away for the weekend." Shuffle put his paws over his eyes.

"Pull yourself together, pug," I barked. "Where did Ranger Jack catch you?"

"I was coming home from Uptown House," muttered Shuffle. "Walter Barkly left me with Caterina Smith. Lord Red kept bouncing at me, so I started walking home to wait for Walter Barkly."

"So," I said, "Ranger Jack caught you without your collar. Walter Barkly wasn't home, so he called Sarge on the terrier-phone to come and get you."

"That's right," snuffled Shuffle. "The pound is full. The pug-mugger's taken so many collars that there are a lot of dogs waiting for their owners."

"Pug-mugger? What pug-mugger?"

"Pug-muggers mug pugs and other dogs and steal their collars," said Shuffle.

"Hmm," I said. I hadn't known this, but I wasn't going to admit this fact to Shuffle.

I decided right then that I'd take the case.

Jack's Glossary

Pupular. *Popular, only used for dogs.*

Pawmission. *Permission, only used for dogs.*

In-terrier-gation. *Same as interrogation, but done by a terrier.*

Pawfect. *Perfect, only used for dogs.*

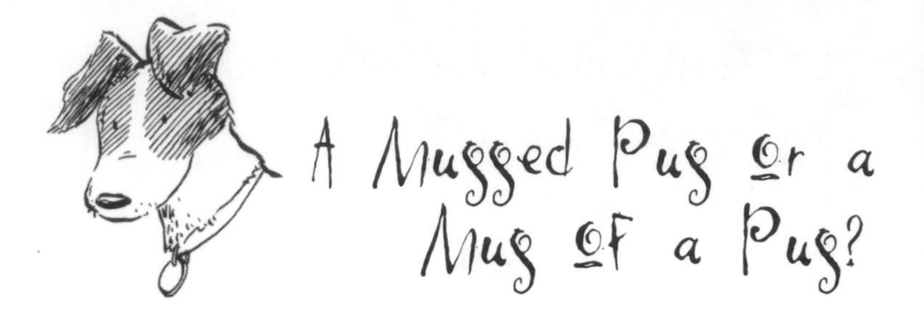

A Mugged Pug Or a Mug Of a Pug?

Shuffle said he'd been pug-mugged just before Ranger Jack arrived.

"Sure you didn't just lose your collar?" I asked. "Maybe you caught it on a branch when you were leaving Uptown House."

"Maybe a Jack Russell doesn't know a branch from a pug-mugger. But any pug will tell you – "

"That's enough!" I **jack-yapped**.

That brought Sarge out. I didn't jack-attack his leg this time. I turned my back and sniffed, to let him know he was still in the **doghouse**.

That's when I smelled something interesting.

I did a quick **nose map**.

Jack's map:

1. Beef cooking in the kitchen.

2. My blanket that Auntie Tidge knitted for me.

3. Foxie.

4. Auntie Tidge baking special biscuits.

5. Sarge's coffee steaming.

Hmm, it wasn't any of those.

"What's all the noise about, Jack?" asked Sarge.

Sniff-sniff. I focused my **super-sniffer** on Shuffle.

6. My collar.

7. Shuffle.

8. Lord Red.
9. Caterina Smith.
10. Ranger Jack.
11. A stranger.

Hmm. I sniff-sniffed again. A plan was forming in my mind, but I needed my collar to carry it out. **Flea soap**! I needed my collar in any case.

I didn't want to forgive Sarge yet, but Jack Russell, Dog Detective, isn't a dog to let a grudge stand in the way of a good lead, so I did the **paw thing** to show Sarge what I wanted.

Sarge laughed. "Oh, all right, Jack." He unbuckled my collar from Shuffle's neck. "I guess you won't be needing a collar in our yard, boy," he said to Shuffle. "And from what Ranger Jack says, you're not the only dog without a collar in Doggeroo."

He buckled the collar on me, and I gave him a quick jack-attack as a reward. I had my collar – my pawfect, comfy collar. I also had backup for Shuffle's statement that dogs were losing collars. "Stay here," I said to Shuffle.

"Where are you going, Jack?"

"To interview a witness," I said. "Either you really have been **collared**, mugged, and de-collared, or else you're just a mug of a pug."

Jack's Facts

Garden fences are to keep other dogs out, not to keep Jacks in.
Jacks jump over.

Jacks burrow under.
Jacks squirm through.
This is a fact.

I left the garden (never mind how) and headed for Uptown House. On the way, I saw three Squekes doing what Squekes do in Dora Barkins' yard.

"Are you wearing collars?" I asked sternly.

"What's it to you, Jack?" yaffled the Squekes.

"Answer in the name of the paw!" I said. "Are you wearing your collars?"

The Squekes flew at the gate, yaffling. Their hair blew back in the wind and I saw their old brown collars. A formal interview was not necessary. I had to see Lord Red.

Jack's Glossary

Jack-yap. *Shrill, very loud yap, yapped by a Jack.*

Doghouse. *For a person to be in a doghouse is a disgrace. For a dog, it's pawfectly fine.*

Jack's Glossary

Nose map. *Way of storing information collected by the nose.*

Super-sniffer. *Jack's nose in super-tracking mode.*

Flea soap. *A terrier-able swear word.*

Paw thing. *Up on hind legs, paws held together as if praying. Means pleased excitement.*

Collared. *Grabbed by the collar.*

Red at the Ready

When I reached Uptown House, Lord Red was rushing about, whirling his tail.

"Shuffle, come out now! Shuffle, Shuffle, where are you?" he barked.

"Red, get your paws over here!" I yapped.

"Jack, Jack, is that you Jack? Jack, Jack, come and help me find Shuffle. We are playing hide – "

"Stop that, Red!" I growled. "Shuffle isn't here."

"Yes he is. We're playing hide-and-squeak. Shuffle, Shuffle! Where are you?"

"Halt!" I barked.

Red skidded to a halt. "Yes, Jack? Have you come to play, Jack?"

"I'm on a case," I said.

"Can I help, Jack, please?"

"Settle down," I commanded. "Sit. Stay. Drop."

Red sat, stayed and dropped.

I in-terrier-gated Red, and this is what I learned.

1. Shuffle the pug *had* been staying with Caterina Smith and Red while Walter Barkly was away.
2. Shuffle *had* been wearing a collar when Red last saw him.
3. It was a smart, new, blue leather collar with a silver pug emblem.
4. Red had no idea when Shuffle had left Uptown House.

"He was here just now," said Red. "Has Shuffle disappeared, Jack? Has he been **dognapped**? What can I do?"

I told Red to stand by. "And *don't* lose your collar," I said.

"Never!" said Red. "It's brand new. Besides, Caterina Smith says dogs without collars go to the poooound!"

The pug really had been mugged. Now I had to find the person who had done it.

I trotted home past the showground where the Sunday markets are. As I crossed the overpass, I met a person eating a meat pie. He snapped his fingers to me.

<u>*Jack's Facts*</u>

It pays to approach people eating pies.

People eating pies drop morsels of meat.

Some dogs say pies might be poison.

People don't eat poisoned pies.

This is a fact.

The pie-person gave me a bite of pie, rubbed my neck and told me to run home.

Jack's Glossary

Dognapped. Kidnapped, only done to a dog.

Pink Stink

When I got home, Shuffle was sulking on our porch. There were two big beef bones in front of him. I picked one up. A **jack-snack** is always welcome.

Shuffle sighed.

"Aren't you hungry?" I began to gnaw my bone.

"I'm too sad." Shuffle put his jaw back on his paws.

"Foxie will guzzle it if you don't watch out," I warned.

"Who cares?" said Shuffle. "What will Walter Barkly say when he finds out I've been mugged?"

"He won't know," I said. "He'll think you lost your collar."

I picked up the other bone and carried it to the corner of the yard. Then I dug a hole and buried it.

Shuffle whined.

"Cheer up," I said. "Jack Russell's the name, detection's the game. I'll get your collar back."

"How?" asked Shuffle.

Jack's Facts

Jacks can do anything.
They don't always know exactly how they're going to do it.
That doesn't mean it won't be done.
This is a fact.

"I need to discuss the case with my second-in-command."

I barked for Foxie to come over.

We waited. No Foxie.

"Foxie!" I barked. "Get your paws over here!"

We waited. No Foxie.

"Looks like your second-in-command's ignoring you," said Shuffle.

"He must be out with Auntie Tidge," I corrected.

I did a quick nose map.

Jack's map:

1. Beef cooling in the kitchen.

2. Fading smell of Auntie Tidge's special biscuits.

3. A whiff of buried beef bone.

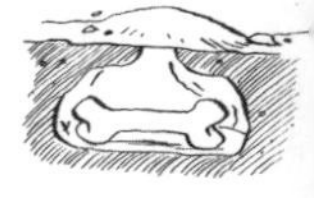

4. Fat Molly Cat from the library trotting up the street.

5. Foxie in Auntie Tidge's garden.

What???

Foxie was just on the other side of the hedge? Ignoring me?

"Foxie, get yourself here, pronto!" I jack-yapped.

We waited. No Foxie.

I trotted over to the hedge. Foxie was definitely there. I could smell him. I sniff-sniffed, and smelled something else. A **pink stink.**

I **jack-jumped** so I could see over the hedge.

There was Foxie, hiding under a bush.

"Foxie," I growled. "Get over here."

Foxie crept towards the gap between his terrier-tory and mine.

"What's wrong with him?" asked Shuffle. "Has someone mugged him and stolen his new collar?"

Foxie crawled up to the porch and then rolled over. "*This* is what's wrong," he growled. "Look!"

We looked.

Foxie's belly was bright pink.

Jack's Glossary

Jack-snack. *A snack for a Jack.*

Pink stink. *A smell that is bright pink.*

Jack-jump. *A sudden spring made by a Jack.*

Super-Sniffer

No Jack laughs when a pal's been painted pink. It was just coincidence that I had to go and have a long **jack-lap** from my water bowl.

While I was jack-lapping, Shuffle asked, "What's that?"

Foxie was too ashamed to speak, so I answered for him.

"It's Auntie Tidge's anti-itch lotion," I said. "Foxie was scratching too much."

"So?" grumbled Foxie. "What's so terrier-able about that? I *like* to scratch."

Jack's Facts

Dogs like to scratch.
Humans don't like dogs to scratch.
Too much scratching leads to flea baths
or to being painted pink.
This is a fact.

I told Foxie to scratch in private. Just then Red came tearing along the street.

"Jack, Jack! Jaaaack!"

Foxie, Shuffle, and I scooted down the porch steps. Red sailed over the fencc and landed right on top of my **squeaker-bone**.

"Sorrrry!" yelped Red, and sailed back over the fence.

A few seconds later, he stuck his long nose back into my terrier-tory. "Did

I squash you, Jack? Did I?"

"Do I *look* squashed?"

"You squeaked," said Red.

"My squeaker-bone squeaked," I corrected. "You might as well come in."

Red sailed over the fence for a third time. He stared at Shuffle. "Why are you here, Shuffle? I thought we were playing hide-and-squeak?" Then he stared at Foxie. "Why is your belly pink, Foxie? Is

Jack investigating your case?"

"Foxie's pink belly has no bearing on the case, Red," I said.

Well, that's what I thought at the time.

"Won't Caterina Smith be looking for you?" I added.

"Caterina Smith is looking for Shuffle down at the reserve," said Red. "I got lonely after Caterina Smith left. That's why I came to see you, Jack. And do you know what, Jack? I nearly lost my new collar on the way!"

"How could you *nearly* lose your collar?" asked Shuffle.

"I was running past the showground when a kind man stopped me. He said my collar was loose. It's new, and the silver thing hadn't gone into the leather thing properly. He fixed it for me." Red's eyes gleamed. "Wasn't that kind of him? He said I was a good doggie!"

I jack-jumped up to check his smart new collar.

"It's not loose now, Jack," said Red.

"No," I said. "It isn't even there! Your *kind man* was really the pug-mugger!"

"But he *helped* me with my lovely new collar, Jack!" Red said.

"He was *mugging* you," I said. "You *know* not to play with strangers!"

"Of course," said Red. "Caterina Smith says I might get dognapped. But he wasn't a dognapper."

"He mugged you and stole your collar," said Shuffle.

"He *fixed* my collar," insisted Red. "The silver thing didn't fit in the leather thing because it's so new! Why would he steal my collar? I'm worth a fistful of dollars. Who would steal my collar and not dognap *me*?"

This case was getting complicated.

I jack-yapped for order. "We have a suspect now," I said, "and two witnesses."

"Who, Jack? Are you going to in-terrier-gate them, Jack? Can I help, Jack?"

"Not unless you want to in-terrier-gate yourself, Red," I said. "You're one witness. Shuffle is the other."

"I'm a victim, not a witness!" snapped Shuffle. "I'm a mugged pug!"

"A victim can also be a witness," I explained. (I've heard Sarge say that.) "You must cast your minds back."

"Are you going to **yip-notize** us, Jack?" asked Red. "Are you?"

"No," I said. "Tell me everything you

remember about the pug-mugger."

Shuffle said the pug-mugger was big. Red said he wasn't. Shuffle said he'd growled at the mugger. Red said that he hadn't.

"Maybe he was nice to you because you've got big teeth," I said to Red. "Unless there are *two* muggers."

I used my super-sniffer. First, I sniff-sniffed Shuffle. The smell of the pug-mugger was fading, because Shuffle had been with Ranger Jack and with Sarge.

But there was still a faint trace. I sniff-sniffed to fix it in my **smellbank**.

Then I checked Red for the same trace. Red squirmed and complained I was messing up his ears. Foxie threatened to swing off them instead.

"You'll make me all pink!" protested Red.

"The pink only comes off when it's wet," snarled Foxie. "Otherwise, you'd be wearing it already."

While Foxie was explaining the pink stink, I finished sniff-sniffing Red. Success! "I can dogmatically state," I announced, "that the pug-mugger who attacked Shuffle is the *same* mugger who stole Red's collar."

I waited for **appaws**, but the others were staring – Shuffle and Foxie through the gate and Red over the gate.

Their ears (and mine) had picked up a familiar cry.

"Lordie, *Lordie*! Lordieeeeee!"

"Here comes Caterina Smith," said Red. He sailed over the gate for a fourth time, and **greeted** Caterina Smith. Then he sailed over the gate for the fifth time.

He landed on my squeaker-bone, again.

Caterina Smith dashed through the gate. "Lordie, you naughty, *naughty* boy! Shuffle, what are you doing here? I've been looking for you everywhere!"

Sarge came out to see what was going on. Sarge might not be the brightest biscuit in the box, but he knows trouble when he smells it.

"Calm down, Caterina," he said. "What's going on?"

"Why didn't you call and tell me Lordie and Shuffle were here?" snapped Caterina Smith. "Walter Barkly left him with me and he disappeared! I went pug-hunting and then Lordie disappeared. Now they've lost their collars!"

"I didn't know Shuffle was meant to

be at your house," said Sarge. "As for Lordie, he's just arrived. Now you can take them both home. We could put Jack's collar back on Shuffle, and maybe Foxie's will..."

I didn't wait for Sarge to finish, and neither did Foxie. Both of us shot out of the yard (never mind how) and went to hide under Auntie Tidge's bed.

Jack's Glossary

Jack-lap. *A drink lapped out of a water bowl by a Jack.*

Squeaker-bone. *Item for exercising a Jack's jaws. Not to be confused with a toy.*

Jack's Glossary

Yip-notize. To *hypnotize, as practiced by a terrier.*

Smellbank. *A dog's collection of remembered smells.*

Appaws. *Cheering and paw-prancing to praise a clever act.*

Greeted. *This is done by rising to the hind legs and clutching a person with the paws while slurping them up the face.*

Jack on the Track

Sarge drove Caterina Smith, Lord Red and Shuffle back to Uptown House.

As soon as they left, Foxie and I crawled out from under Auntie Tidge's bed.

"If we're quick, we might be able to track the pug-mugger," I said.

I sniffed the air a few times to clear my smellbank, and then put my super-sniffer to work on a quick nose map.

Jack's map:

1. Fat Molly sunning herself on a wall.

2. The three Squekes playing with a dehydrated rat.

3. Dora Barkins' sheepskin coat.

4. The buried beef bone.

5. Sarge's cold coffee.

6. A whiff of biscuit
   from Auntie Tidge.

7. The pink stink on Foxie.

8. Six sparrows squabbling
   under a bush.

9. Red's pawprints.

Some dogs might have wasted time tracking Fat Molly or the rat, or **terrierizing** the sparrows, but not a tracking Jack. My super-sniffer fixed on the right scent and I began to track.

With Foxie trotting after me, I tracked my way past the three Squekes and turned right towards the showground.

Sniff-sniff, sniff-sniff, I followed Red's original trail. The closer we got to the showground, the stronger the trace of the pug-mugger became.

When we were near the overpass, even Foxie could smell it.

"He went *this* way," I said.

Sniff-sniff, sniff-sniff. Red-scent, pug-mugger-scent.

"Hey Jack!" yapped Foxie. "Wait!"

Sniff-sniff, sniff-sniff. Red-scent, pug-mugger-scent, pie-person-scent. I tracked on.

Jack's Facts

A tracking Jack never leaves the trail.
A tracking Jack takes no notice of anything **but** *the trail.*
This is mostly a fact.

The pie-person-scent got stronger. This was a problem. A really strong pie-smell can distract even a tracking Jack. Suddenly, pie-person was all I could smell. He was on the overpass, eating another pie.

I stopped, and sniff-sniffed. Foxie was drooling.

"You again, Jack?" asked the pie-person. "Off you go."

Some people understand about tracking Jacks. The pie-person could see I was busy with a case. As I sniff-sniffed on, I heard guzzling behind me.

Foxie was feasting.

Foxie used to be a street dog. He *never* passes up a snack.

I tracked on.

When I reached the showground, the pug-mugger-scent had faded.

"That's odd," I said.

"What's odd?" Foxie trotted up beside me, licking his chops.

"The mugger – " I stared at Foxie. "Foxie, where's your collar?"

"My *collar*?" Foxie scratched at his neck with his claw. "It's fallen off."

"**Dogwash**!" I said. "It was a new one. It was bright red and shiny."

Foxie turned three times, trying to see his neck. Then he gave up and sat down.

Quickly, I nose-mapped Foxie.

1. Foxie.
2. Pink stink.
3. Meat pie.
4. Auntie Tidge.
5. Special biscuit
6. The mugger.

Foxie had definitely been in contact with the mugger, but where? When?

"I've got it!" I yapped. "I've cracked the case!"

I waited for appaws, but Foxie just looked **foxed**.

"The pie-person!" I explained. "The pie-person is the mugger. Don't you see, Foxie? He stole your collar while you were guzzling pie!"

"Dogwash," said Foxie. "Red and Shuffle never mentioned pies."

"He uses different methods for different victims," I said. "Shuffle's easy to grab, so the mugger grabbed him. Red is easy to trick, so the mugger pretended to help him. You're easy to bribe, so he bribed you with pie."

"What about *you*, Jack?" snarled Foxie.

"He could see there's no point bribing me," I said.

"Or maybe you're just not worth mugging?" Foxie sneered.

"We both met the pie-person-pug-mugger," I said, "and which of us still has his collar?"

I knew we were on the right track now. We had a suspect. We knew he could have mugged the dogs of Doggeroo. What we didn't know was *why*. To find out, we raced back to the overpass, but the suspect had gone.

"He's not getting away with this," I stated.

We picked up his scent and tracked the suspect to the library. Fat Molly was washing herself on the step. She called us something rude in **catspeak**, but we took no notice. We tracked to the police station. Then we tracked up the hill to the other showground entrance near the Sunday markets.

People were setting up stalls already.

That's where we sniffed down the suspect. We hid behind a corn dog stand and watched him unloading things from a van.

I wanted to terrier-ize him into giving us back the collars, but terrier-izing people gets terriers into trouble. Besides, it isn't as easy as you might think.

Jack's Facts

Jacks are brave.
Jacks are bold.
Jacks are not the biggest dogs in the world.
Some people don't take them seriously.
This is a fact.

"Will Sarge arrest him?" asked Foxie.

"Maybe, but first we need to set up a **doggo obbo**," I decided. "We need to find out where the suspect is hiding the collars. We also need his motive."

"Maybe he has a lot of dogs?" suggested Foxie. "Why else would he steal Red's collar and my collar, but not Red and me?"

I looked at him. "What dognapper

would want you, Foxie?"

"Or you?" snapped Foxie. "This one didn't even want your silly old collar!"

My hackles rose, but now wasn't the time to fight with Foxie. We had some **skulldoggery** to stop.

Our doggo obbo didn't last long. Ranger Jack came in one showground gate, so we slipped out the other. We couldn't risk him catching Foxie without his collar. Besides, it was dinnertime.

Jack's Facts

Doggo obbos are important.
So is avoiding Ranger Jack.
Dinner is the most important thing of all.
This is a fact.

Jack's Glossary

Terrier-izing. *Frightening.*

Dogwash. *Nonsense!*

Foxed. *Puzzled, as only a fox terrier can be.*

Catspeak. *The way cats talk.*

Doggo obbo. *An observation carried out by dogs.*

Skulldoggery. *Something bad concerning dogs.*

Steak-Out

Auntie Tidge was cross that Foxie had lost his collar. So Foxie had to be fast on his feet to join me at the doggo obbo next morning. We arranged a **steak-out** behind the corn dog stand.

At first, everything was quiet. Then the suspect came out of the van and began to set up his stall. He laid out watches, pens, and other small things. Then he laid out some dog collars. They all had blue tags.

We were about to fetch Sarge to make an arrest, when Caterina Smith walked past the corn dog stand. She approached the suspect.

"Bother!" I said. "She'll find Red's collar. Then she'll get the credit for solving *my* case!"

Caterina Smith picked up some collars. She shook her head and put them down again. The suspect fetched another bunch of collars from the van. These had yellow tags.

Caterina Smith took one. She smiled. She gave the suspect some money and went back up the hill to Uptown House.

"What's going on?" I asked. "Why didn't she recognize Red's collar?"

Foxie scratched his belly even though Auntie Tidge had re-pinked him. "Would *you* recognize Red's collar?"

"Of course," I said. "It smells like Red."

Gloria Smote came by, carrying Polly the dachshund. Polly snarled at the suspect, and struggled to get down.

"Naughty!" said Gloria Smote. "You can't get down without your collar. You know what Ranger Jack said."

She bought a collar from the suspect.

"That's not Polly's collar," I said.

Gloria Smote put the collar on Polly, and carried her away.

During the first hour of our steak-out, we saw Jill Russell, and three other dogs I didn't know. All their people bought collars from the suspect.

Could I be barking up the wrong tree? Could the suspect be innocent?

No. There was evidence against him. He *must* have stolen Foxie's collar.

I left the steak-out and trotted over to the suspect's stall. I sniff-sniffed about. I was *sure* I could smell Foxie's collar. And Red's. And Polly's collar, too.

I jack-jumped so I could see the collars on the stall.

"You again, Jack!" said the suspect. "What do you want?"

"He's shopping for a new collar," said the corn dog man.

I jack-jumped again, and sniff-sniffed. I could still smell Foxie's collar, but I couldn't see it.

I went back to Foxie. "I can tell you one thing," I said. "These collars aren't brand new."

"Where's my collar?" asked Foxie.

"I think the Doggeroo collars are stashed in the van. Which means . . . well, you know what *that* means, Foxie!"

It meant I had all the facts I needed to make an arrest. We knew the guilty person.

We knew he had used force, trickery and bribery .

"And we even know *why* he did it," I told Foxie.

"Do we?" asked Foxie.

I sighed.

Sometimes, Foxie just isn't entirely **on the ball**!

Jack's Glossary

Steak-out. *A place where detectives can watch suspects and eat at the same time.*

On the ball. *Dogs chase balls. Clever dogs always jump on them to stop them rolling.*

Jack-pack Attack

"The suspect has been clever," I said. "If he hadn't come to Doggeroo, he might have gone on mugging pugs (and bribing fox terriers and fooling setters) forever."

"Here's what I think he's been doing. One: the pug-mugger goes to Town One and steals smart collars. Two: he moves to Town Two and steals more collars. Three: in Town Two, he sells the collars from Town One to the people whose dogs he mugged in Town Two. Four: he moves to Town Three and steals more collars. Five: he sells the collars from Town Two to the people whose dogs he mugged in Town Three; and so on."

I sat back and waited for appaws.

Instead, Foxie scratched his ribs. "So that's why he didn't mug *you*, Jack. Nobody would want *your* old collar."

"*I* want my collar!" I snapped. "It's special. Sarge gave it to me."

"And I want mine!" snarled Foxie. "Mine is special. Auntie Tidge gave it to me."

I sighed. I'd solved the case, but that didn't get the collars back.

"I think this calls for backup from the **jack-pack**," I said.

"Run round the market and alert all the dogs you can find," I told Foxie. "I'll get Red and Shuffle and the Squekes.

We need lots of fuss and yaffle. *Nobody* can yaffle like the Squekes."

Foxie trotted off, and I ran to Uptown House. Red was playing hide-and-squeak by himself. Shuffle was snuffling under a bush.

"Jack, Jack, I've got another collar!" barked Red. "And Jack, do you know what, Jack? My new collar smells just like the kind man who took my other collar. Isn't that funny, Jack?"

Jack's Facts

Most dogs are brighter than you think. A few of them are dimmer than you would believe.
This is a fact.

"Not very," I said. "He stole your collar to sell, and he's sold Caterina Smith one that belonged to someone else. He's still got yours. And we have to find it."

"Can I help you find it, Jack? Can I?"

"What about mine?" asked Shuffle.

"He's still got yours, too," I said. "Come on! We're going to get them back!"

Red sailed over the fence. Shuffle crammed himself through a gap. (Never mind how it got there.) I sent Shuffle straight to the showground. Red and I dashed around Doggeroo calling for backup.

Did it work? Of course it did! No Doggeroo dog would miss the chance to run with the jack-pack! In half an hour the jack-pack was trotting towards the showground. Three minutes after that, fifty-nine dogs dodged through the market and gathered at the corn dog stand. We were almost ready to storm the suspect's stall.

"What are we waiting for?" yaffled the Squekes.

"Wait!" I jack-yapped.

I cocked my ears. Any minute now...

"Lordie, *Lordie*! Lordieeeeee!"

"Polly, you come back here!"

"Jill, Jill! Oh, you *naughty* dog!"

"Lordie, *Lordie*! Lordieeeeee!"

"Foxie-woxie, Jackie-wackie!"

"Jack? Where are you?"

"That's what we're waiting for!" I said.

Our people came rushing (and puffing) towards the corn dog stand. Caterina Smith was in the lead, followed by Gloria Smote and Dora Barkins. Sarge was making pretty good speed. Panting along behind him was Auntie Tidge.

At the back came Ranger Jack.

"Jack-pack! ATTACK!" I ordered. We launched ourselves at the suspect's stall.

Jack's Glossary

Jack-pack. *A noble pack of dogs united under a strong leader.*

The Pink-stink Plan

We didn't hurt the suspect. Jack-pack attacks are all about noise and attracting backup. Some of us ran round and round the stall. This stopped the suspect from escaping. Some of us gathered around the van. This showed the backup people where to look.

I sniff-sniffed to make sure the goods were still inside.

They were.

The Squekes yaffled. Red sailed over the stall. Jill and Polly and Shuffle milled around. It was a sea of dogs, a posse of pups! It was all part of the plan.

Foxie sneaked into the corn dog stand and ate three corn dogs.

That *wasn't* part of the plan.

"Jack, what *is* this?" Sarge sounded a bit annoyed.

This was my big moment. I sniffed loudly at the van, and then did the paw thing.

Sarge looked sternly at the suspect. "I'm Sergeant Russell," he said, "of the Doggeroo Police."

"Oh," said the suspect.

"Is this your van, sir?" asked Sarge. "Can you explain what my dog finds so interesting about it?"

The suspect looked at me. "You *again*, Jack?" He sighed. "What kind of

place has police dogs going undercover as Jack Russell terriers?"

That was almost the end of The Case of the Mugged Pug. The suspect gave back the Doggeroo collars. Sarge took the rest of the stock into custody.

It wasn't quite the end, though. Catching a criminal is one thing. Preventing crime is even more important. I had a plan to make sure no one ever stole another Doggeroo dog collar.

"How will we do that, Jack?" asked Red.

"We'll mark the collars," I said. "Foxie? Think you can steal the pink-stink lotion from Auntie Tidge's cupboard?"